HABITAT HAVOC

URBAN SPRAWL

By Barbara Linde

Gareth Stevens
Publishing

A NOT-SO-SCENIC VIEW

Imagine this: You're flying to a large city. You've been looking out the window at the rolling farmland and majestic forests. You think about all the crops that are growing. You picture the wild animals that are living in the forests.

Suddenly, the scene changes. The farmland and forests end. In their place, you see mile after mile of houses, shopping malls, and parking lots. Roads wind among the houses. There's hardly any green space. It's the same in every direction, as far as you can see. You're looking at **urban** sprawl.

An Old Problem

Urban sprawl can be traced all the way back to Rome, when poorer citizens lived outside the city walls since too many people lived inside. Big US cities, such as Boston, Massachusetts, and New York City, started sprawling in the late 1800s and early 1900s. Immigrants living in crowded city neighborhoods were finally able to afford to move out—so they did.

The **suburban** area around Chicago, Illinois, is so big that together with the city it's sometimes called the "Chicagoland" area.

WHAT IS A HABITAT?

A habitat is a place where an animal or plant lives and grows. For example, a tree could house robins in a nest, a family of squirrels, and a colony of ants at its roots.

Very often, our actions can affect habitats all over the world. While problems like pollution harm plants and animals, it's the **destruction** of different habitats that really hurts their populations. Urban sprawl is one major way habitat loss occurs. When **developing** land, companies cut down forests to clear land for building, fill in **wetlands**, and pave over soil that would be good for farming.

Then and Now

The chart shows the population and land area of four of the largest **metropolitan** areas in the United States. Look at the changes from 1950 to 2013.

city, state	population, 1950	population, 2013	land area, 1950	land area, 2013
New York, New York	7.9 million	20.7 million	315 sq miles (816 sq km)	4,495 sq miles (11,642 sq km)
Los Angeles, California	1.9 million	15 million	450 sq miles (1,165 sq km)	2,432 sq miles (6,299 sq km)
Chicago, Illinois	3.6 million	9.1 million	207 sq miles (536 sq km)	2,647 sq miles (6,856 sq km)
Houston, Texas	596,163	5.4 million	160 sq miles (414 sq km)	1,793 sq miles (4,644 sq km)

When people build homes in the suburbs, businesses—such as restaurants and grocery stores—have to be built nearby, too. This removes even more habitats.

WHAT IS URBAN SPRAWL?

Urban sprawl is the fast geographic growth of cities and towns. Sometimes a growing population causes it, while in other places people just want more space and bigger homes.

Though suburbs have been growing around US cities since the late 1800s, many sprang up following World War I. By the 1920s, it was common for families to live in single-family homes in suburbs. Then, after World War II, the government started a loan program that made it easy for families to buy homes and cars. Demand for suburban homes and businesses grew. However, cities often didn't plan the growth well, and habitats around them suffered.

The Interstate Highway System

President Franklin D. Roosevelt first recognized the need for a high-speed highway system connecting cities in the United States in the 1930s. However, it was President Dwight D. Eisenhower's signing of the Federal Aid Highway Act of 1956 that finally put into motion a plan for building the Interstate Highway System. The system now has more than 45,000 miles (72,405 km) of highway all over the country.

You can see here how the city of Denver, Colorado, is spreading out.

Interstate Highway plan, 1955

LEGEND

Interstate System urban routes
designated in September 1955

O Urban areas served

FAREWELL, FARMS AND FORESTS

Each year, more than 2 million acres (810,000 ha) of open land, including farms and forests, are swallowed up by urban sprawl. Open farmland and forests help keep air and water clean, and they're beautiful to look at. They help prevent flooding and **erosion**. Wild animals make their homes and find food on farms and in forests.

But as more people move to the suburbs, farmers sell their land. Forests have to be cleared for construction. Animals may have nowhere to go. In some cases, habitat destruction can cause an animal to become **endangered** or to die out altogether.

Saving Farms

Groups such as the American Farmland Trust are trying to save farmland across the United States. They argue that farming employs many Americans and contributes about $1 trillion to the economy. In addition, **environmentalists** say that pollution caused by urban development is made worse by the loss of farmland, since farmland helps remove waste from both air and water.

Farmland is needed to grow crops, but that's not the only reason it's important. Farms can be home to many different kinds of plants and animals.

WETLAND WOES

Wetlands help control floods and reduce water pollution by removing harmful matter and dirt. They're also important habitats that are often home to hundreds of species of plants and animals. However, wetlands are drained and then filled in to build suburban neighborhoods. The plants and animals lose their habitats, and water quality worsens.

The Everglades are more than 4,300 square miles (11,137 sq km) of marshy land in southern Florida. Though that sounds large, the Everglades used to be twice as big! Much of their land has been lost to suburbs. This harms populations of animals that only live there, such as the Florida panther.

Impermeable Surfaces

Impermeable surfaces, such as sidewalks and roads, are a big problem of urban sprawl. When it rains, the water doesn't soak into them the way it would soak into wetlands or soil. Flooding can become more common. Harmful chemicals, dirt, and trash are more easily carried into local streams and rivers, polluting them.

In recent years, laws protecting the Everglades have been passed. However, they cannot undo damage that has already been done.

Map labels:

Orlando
Kissimmee
Tampa
St. Petersburg
Chain of Lakes
Kissimmee
Port St. Lucie
St. Lucie
Gulf of Mexico
Lake Okeechobee
Caloosahatchee
West Palm Beach
Cape Coral
Loxahatchee NWR
Ft. Lauderdale
Naples
Big Cypress NP
The Everglades
Hialeah
Ten Thousand Islands
Miami
Biscayne NP
Homestead
Everglades NP
Cape Sable
Florida Bay
Key West
Atlantic Ocean

0   20   40 Miles
0   25   50 Kilometers

River
Canal
Swamp/Marsh
• City: 15,000 to 150,000 pop.
● City: 150,000 or greater pop.
Urbanized Area
County
South Florida WMD
Water Conservation Area
Everglades Agricultural Area
National Park
National Preserve
National Wildlife Refuge
Indian Reservation
National Marine Sanctuary

DESERT DIFFICULTIES

Urban sprawl is taking over desert habitats in the southwestern United States. Cities sprawling into the desert include Phoenix and Tucson, Arizona, and Los Angeles, California. The city and suburbs of Las Vegas, Nevada, were the fastest growing metropolitan area in the country throughout the 1990s.

A City with a Plan

In 1997, Tucson wanted to build a school in a habitat of the endangered pygmy owl. The debate this sparked ended up having a big impact! The Sonoran Desert Conservation Plan set aside land to protect the owl as well as other animals in the desert habitat around the city. The plan allowed for city growth, too, but it's monitored closely.

Sprawl in the desert affects the famous desert plant, the cactus. Ants, birds, and box turtles all eat different parts of the cactus. When cacti are destroyed to build suburbs, the animals may starve. Owls, woodpeckers, and other birds make their nests in the tall saguaro (suh-WAHR-uh) cactus of the Sonoran Desert. Where will they live if the cacti are gone?

saguaro cactus

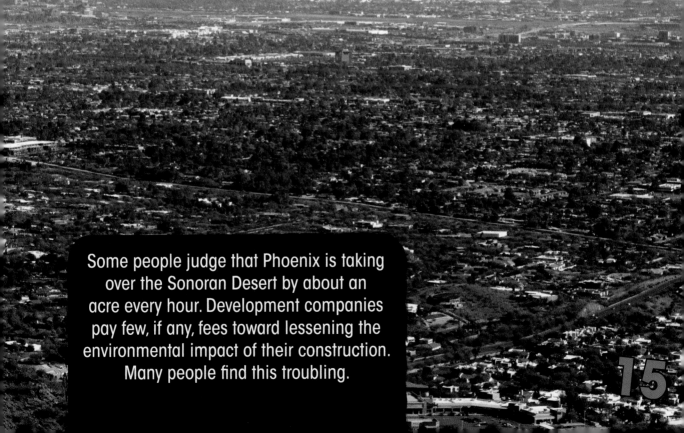

Some people judge that Phoenix is taking over the Sonoran Desert by about an acre every hour. Development companies pay few, if any, fees toward lessening the environmental impact of their construction. Many people find this troubling.

CITY COYOTES

What do animals do when urban sprawl reaches their habitat? Some, like the coyote, stay and adapt.

Urban sprawl is good for coyotes in some ways. They're safe from large predators, and food is easy to get from garbage cans and even dishes of pet food left outside. Scientists who study these animals say their populations have risen in the last few decades, perhaps because of urban living.

Many coyotes have been spotted in Los Angeles and Chicago, Illinois, as well as Washington, DC. They eat small animals like rats, mice, and squirrels, keeping the populations of these pests down.

The Bad News

Coyotes have been known to hunt pets that have been left alone outside. They've attacked several people trying to protect their pets, too. Most of the time, urban coyotes stay away from people. But as they continue to live side by side with us in cities, they'll become less afraid of people, which could cause more problems in the future.

Coyotes have been seen crossing streets, walking over bridges, and resting in urban parks. Though they're sharing a habitat with people, it's important to remember that they're still wild animals.

GROUCHY GRIZZLIES

Many animals aren't able to adapt to urban sprawl. Grizzly bears die at a greater rate the closer they are to where people are building and living. Roads and homes split up their natural territory, making it harder for them to find food and places to live. Hungry bears may then raid peoples' garbage cans. This is both scary for people and bad for bears that might get used to people food.

One grizzly bear habitat that's presently facing damaging urban sprawl is near Yellowstone National Park. It's home to the largest population of grizzlies in the lower 48 US states. As more homes and roads are built, that could change, however.

Grizzly bear populations decreased as more people moved to the northwestern United States and Canada. In 1975, they were close to becoming endangered.

Endangered Grizzlies

Around 200 years ago, there were about 50,000 grizzly bears in the United States. As people began to settle in the western United States, the grizzly bear populations fell. In 1975, there were only about 1,000 grizzly bears left! Today, about 58,000 live across Alaska, the northwestern United States, and Canada.

ALLIGATOR ALERT

About 1 million alligators live in Florida's lakes and rivers. Over time, golf courses and shopping malls have replaced many of the places where the gators used to sunbathe and nest. That hasn't stopped alligators. It's not all that unusual for a person to find an alligator on the lawn or even in the swimming pool! They're even seen walking down the road.

However, if someone reports an alligator that's **threatening** them or a pet, a trapper has to be called in. If the gator seems dangerous enough, it's killed. Thousands die this way every year. Why? Alligators have attacked people and pets.

Staying Safe

Since urban sprawl has brought alligators and people closer together, it's important to know how to be safe. Alligators feed at dusk or later at night. If you know there are alligators in the area, stay indoors. Don't let pets or children outside alone. Back slowly away if you get too close to one. Never, ever feed an alligator.

American alligator in Okefenokee Swamp in Georgia

The number of injuries and deaths due to alligator bites varies from year to year. In Florida in 2012, there were seven bites reported, only two of which were thought to be "major." In 2006, though, there were 12 bites and 3 deaths.

TROUBLES FOR THE FISHER

Fishers are part of the weasel family. They're small but fierce hunters. They eat porcupines, birds, and rabbits. The fisher is having a hard time due to urban sprawl.

Fishers' only habitat is the forests of the northern United States and Canada. Suburban neighborhoods are now being built, splitting their habitat into smaller parts. That makes it hard for fishers to travel easily and find shelter in hollow trees and logs. When the forest is destroyed, fishers' food source is also destroyed. They have a hard time finding enough food.

forest cleared for building

Adapting to Split Forests

The populations of some forest animals grow when their habitats are split up by urban sprawl! White-tailed deer, raccoons, opossums, pigeons, squirrels, and skunks have all adapted. They eat some of the same foods as the fisher does, so there's not always enough food for the fisher.

Fishers most often make their homes in thick forests and don't like open spaces. This is a problem when forests in their range are cleared for development or farming.

PEOPLE PROBLEMS

Urban sprawl affects our habitat, too! Because suburbs have little public transportation and many roads, people drive a lot. This causes more air pollution. People may also spend long hours in their cars driving into and out of the city.

The growth of suburbs has left many urban neighborhoods nearly empty. Abandoned buildings aren't kept up, becoming eyesores for anyone left in the neighborhoods.

The United States isn't the only country with this problem. London, England, has been sprawling since before most US cities, while the suburbs of Paris, France, have been growing mostly since the 1920s.

The Megalopolis

The word "megalopolis" comes from Greek words that mean "very large city." It's a group of really big cities and suburbs with not much green space between them. One megalopolis stretches from Boston, Massachusetts, to Washington, DC, including New York City. Others extend from Chicago, Illinois, to Pittsburgh, Pennsylvania, and from San Francisco to San Diego, California.

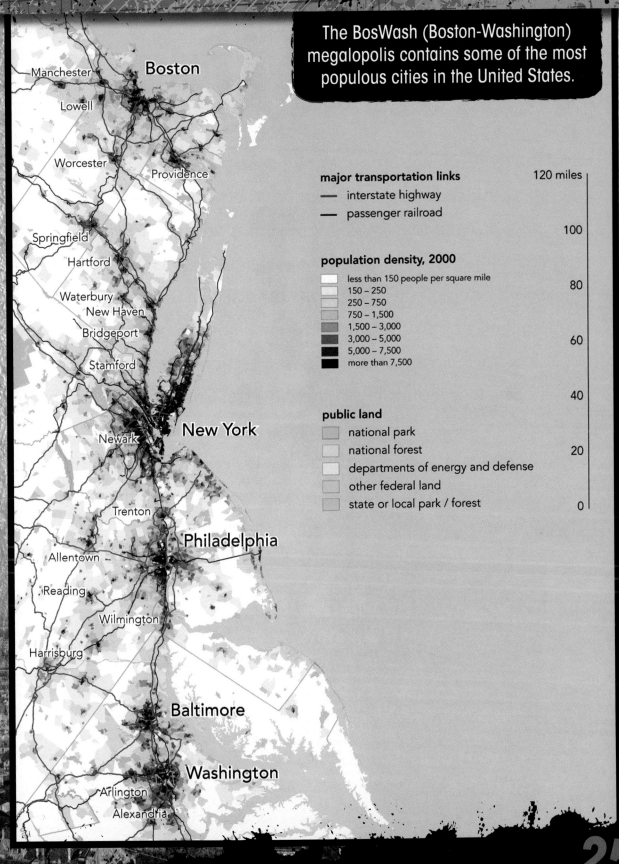

The BosWash (Boston-Washington) megalopolis contains some of the most populous cities in the United States.

Manchester
Lowell
Boston
Worcester
Providence
Springfield
Hartford
Waterbury
New Haven
Bridgeport
Stamford
Newark
New York
Trenton
Philadelphia
Allentown
Reading
Wilmington
Harrisburg
Baltimore
Washington
Arlington
Alexandria

major transportation links

— interstate highway
— passenger railroad

population density, 2000

less than 150 people per square mile
150 – 250
250 – 750
750 – 1,500
1,500 – 3,000
3,000 – 5,000
5,000 – 7,500
more than 7,500

public land

national park
national forest
departments of energy and defense
other federal land
state or local park / forest

120 miles

100

80

60

40

20

0

FOR OR AGAINST?

You've read that urban sprawl destroys wildlife habitats, increases air and water pollution, and covers some of the beautiful open land in our country. But is urban sprawl ever a good thing?

Some people say yes! They like having more living space, both in their homes and yards. Many times, homes and buildings for businesses may be newer than in a city. Housing often costs less than living in the city, too. Crime rates tend to be lower in the suburbs, which draws families looking for safety.

Environmentalists disagree. They don't want to trade animal habitats and land for shopping malls and parking lots. What do you think?

Keep in Mind Both Sides

Environmental groups are often against urban sprawl. People living in a city might not want suburbs built, either. These people may not like the way they look and want to make their neighborhood better instead. Construction and land companies are often in favor of sprawl. So are people who want to live in the suburbs.

Often, those for and against a new suburban project will speak out at town meetings, in letters to the newspaper, and maybe even through protests!

SPRAWL is NOT PROGRESS

SMART SOLUTIONS

Some cities are trying to solve the problems of urban sprawl. This is called urban planning. Here are a few of the ideas:

- limit the size of the space a house can take up;
- build new houses closer together;
- limit the size of a new neighborhood;
- keep some open, or green, space in a neighborhood;
- put in more public transportation from the suburbs to the city;
- put in bicycle and walking paths;
- keep some land safe from building;
- protect native plants and wildlife;
- fix up old urban neighborhoods;
- encourage people to carpool.

Oregon's Success

The state of Oregon has successfully slowed sprawl. In 1973, a law required all cities to establish an Urban Growth Boundary. No homes, malls, businesses, or parking lots could be built beyond that border. This means every construction decision must be purposeful and planned, instead of sprawling.

Cities can grow wisely, without creating sprawl and havoc.

Glossary

destruction: the state of being destroyed or ruined

develop: to create, grow, or change over time

endangered: in danger of dying out

environmentalist: someone concerned with the care of the natural world

erosion: the wearing away of something by wind or water

impermeable: not allowing passage through, watertight

metropolitan: having to do with a city and its surrounding suburbs

suburban: having to do with an area close to the outer edge of a city

threaten: present a danger to

urban: having to do with a city

wetlands: areas that have standing water on the surface for at least part of the year

For More Information

Books

Amsel, Sheri. *The Everything Kids' Environment Book: Learn How You Can Help the Environment by Getting Involved at School, at Home, or at Play.* Avon, MA: Adams Media, 2007.

Leardi, Jeanette. *Making Cities Green.* New York, NY: Bearport Publishing, 2010.

Steele, Philip. *City.* New York, NY: DK Publishing, 2011.

Websites

How Urban Sprawl Works
geography.howstuffworks.com/terms-and-associations/urban-sprawl1.htm
Read articles about the pros and cons of urban sprawl, and look at photographs.

Urban Sprawl
www.pbs.org/wnet/need-to-know/tag/urban-sprawl/
Watch an online video about the problems of urban sprawl in Phoenix, Arizona.

Urban Sprawl: The Big Picture
science.nasa.gov/science-news/science-at-nasa/2002/11oct_sprawl/
See NASA maps and photographs of urban sprawl.

Index